Hello, Family Members,

Learning to read is one of the most [...] of early childhood. **Hello Reader!** [...] children become skilled readers w[...] [...] readers learn to read by remembering frequently used words like "the," "is," and "and"; by using phonics skills to decode new words; and by interpreting picture and text clues. These books provide both the stories children enjoy and the structure they need to read fluently and independently. Here are suggestions for helping your child *before*, *during*, and *after* reading:

Before

- Look at the cover and pictures and have your child predict what the story is about.
- Read the story to your child.
- Encourage your child to chime in with familiar words and phrases.
- Echo read with your child by reading a line first and having your child read it after you do.

During

- Have your child think about a word he or she does not recognize right away. Provide hints such as "Let's see if we know the sounds" and "Have we read other words like this one?"
- Encourage your child to use phonics skills to sound out new words.
- Provide the word for your child when more assistance is needed so that he or she does not struggle and the experience of reading with you is a positive one.
- Encourage your child to have fun by reading with a lot of expression . . . like an actor!

After

- Have your child keep lists of interesting and favorite words.
- Encourage your child to read the books over and over again. Have him or her read to brothers, sisters, grandparents, and even teddy bears. Repeated readings develop confidence in young readers.
- Talk about the stories. Ask and answer questions. Share ideas about the funniest and most interesting characters and events in the stories.

I do hope that you and your child enjoy this book.

— Francie Alexander
  Reading Specialist,
  Scholastic's Learning Ventures

If you have questions or comments about how children learn to read, please contact Francie Alexander at FrancieAl@aol.com

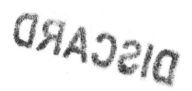

0-439-09978-1

Compilation copyright © 2000 by David McPhail.
A Girl, a Goat, and a Goose and the Feather; A Girl, a Goat, and a Goose and the Storm; A Girl, a Goat, and a Goose Find a Boat; A Girl, a Goat, and a Goose Go for a Ride
Copyright © 2000 by David McPhail.
All rights reserved. Published by Scholastic Inc.
SCHOLASTIC, HELLO READER, CARTWHEEL BOOKS and associated logos are trademarks and/or registered trademarks of Scholastic Inc.

Library of Congress Cataloging-in-Publication Data available

10   03 04

Printed in the U.S.A.
First printing, August 2000

David McPhail

A Girl, a Goat, and a Goose

Hello Reader!—Level 1

SCHOLASTIC INC.

Cartwheel
·B·O·O·K·S·®

New York Toronto London Auckland Sydney Mexico City New Delhi Hong Kong

The Storm

A goose lives
in the little house.
A goat lives in
the bigger house.
A girl lives
in the biggest house.

A cloud comes along.
The sky is dark.
Wind blows
and rain falls.

Lightning flashes
and thunder crashes.
The goose runs
to the goat's house.

"I am afraid,"
says the goose.
"Me, too,"
says the goat.

The goose and
the goat run
to the girl's house.
"We are afraid,"
they tell her.

"Me, too,"
says the girl.
"But with you here,
I am not as afraid."

The girl, the goat,
and the goose
have a party
until the storm is over.

The Feather

The goose has lost
a feather. She looks
all over her house
for it. It is not there.

The goose tells the goat
about the lost feather.
They look all over
the goat's house
for it.
It is not there.

The goose and the goat
tell the girl
about the lost feather.

The goose and the goat
look all over her house.
The girl makes a sign
that reads:

LOST—1 FEATHER
IF FOUND,
PLEASE RETURN TO GOOSE.

"You are writing
with a feather,"
says the goat.

"You are right,"
says the girl.
She gives the feather
to the goose.

Now everyone is happy.

The Ride

The goat has a cart.
The girl and the goose
get in. And off they go.

Here are some cows.
"Hello, cows,"
says the girl.
"Hello, cows,"
says the goat.
The goose says nothing.

Here are some fish.
"Hello, fish," say the girl
and the goat.
The goose says nothing.

Here are some crows.
The girl and the goat
say hello.
The goose does not.

"Why are you so quiet?"
the girl asks the goose.
"Because I can't see
anything," says the goose.

The cart stops.

Then
the cart starts again.
"Now I can see just fine,"
says the goose.

The Boat

A goose, a goat,
and a girl
go to a pond.

The goose swims.
The goat drinks.
The girl catches a fish.

Then
she lets the fish go.

The girl, the goose,
and the goat
sail a boat.

They pretend to sail
across the sea . . .

and all around
the world.

Then
they are back
at the pond
again.